Big Mama and Grandma Ghana

Written by Angela Shelf Medearis

Illustrated by Lynne Russell

SCHOLASTIC INC.

New York   Toronto   London   Auckland   Sydney

Copyright © 1994 by Scholastic Inc.
All rights reserved. Published by Scholastic Inc.
Printed in the U.S.A.
ISBN 0-590-27384-1

9 10   09   00 99 98

23

Big Mama takes care of me
after school. She bakes peanut butter
cookies for me. I lick the bowl.

Big Mama loves to hear me read. Then I tell her all about my day at school. She tells me about the old days when my mom was little.

We play checkers, just like Big Mama and my mom used to. Sometimes I win. Sometimes Big Mama wins. When she loses, she just laughs.

When I eat dinner with Big Mama, she says, "Eat all your greens, Miles. They'll make you strong!" If I eat them all, she gives me a cookie.

My other grandma lives in Ghana, in Africa. She sends me presents when it's my birthday. One night she calls with big news.

"I'm coming to visit you, Miles," Grandma Ghana tells me. "It will be my first visit to America."

"Okay," I say. But I'm a little worried. I wonder what she is like.

Mom, Dad, and I pick up
Grandma Ghana at the airport.
She hugs Dad and Mom.

"Miles," she asks, " can I give
you a hug?" She's my grandma,
so I tell her okay.

Later, we play a counting game Grandma Ghana brought me. We use seeds from Africa. Sometimes I win. Sometimes she wins. When she loses, she just laughs.

"Your daddy and I played
this game when he was your age,"
Grandma Ghana says.

"Did you and Daddy ever see
a wild lion in Africa?" I ask.

"Yes," she says, "in the zoo.
I live in the city, Miles."

We put the game away. Then Grandma Ghana teaches me an Ashanti song. We can hear Dad singing along in the kitchen.

When Big Mama comes, she hugs Grandma Ghana. Then she gives her a big box of peanut butter cookies. Grandma Ghana gives Big Mama an African basket. They both give me a kiss.

We eat African food and
American food for dinner.

"Eat all your greens, Miles,"
Big Mama says.

"They'll make you strong like
a lion," Grandma Ghana says.

Then they smile at each other.

I eat all my greens. Big Mama
gives me one of her peanut butter
cookies. Grandma Ghana smiles
and gives me another cookie. I guess
grandmothers are the same all over
the world.